CHANGE IN FORTUNES

SONNY ANTHONY TUCKER

CHANGE IN FORTUNES

CONTENTS

PREFACE

This is the poignant tale of a young boy, Alimamy Bangalie, whose life is marred by a tragedy he struggles to comprehend. Born into a modest background, Alimamy is the third of three siblings. His father, Mr. Ibrahim Bangalie, is a police officer who ascended the ranks to become a Sergeant, and his mother, Mama Ami, is a dedicated petty trader. Despite her lack of formal education, Mama Ami is unwavering in her commitment to her children's academic and social success.

Alimamy's academic journey began at age ten at St. Edwards Primary School, where he quickly established himself as a standout student, excelling in classes one through four. His academic prowess and friendly nature made him popular among his peers. After school, he would assist his mother in selling kerosene, contributing to the family's well-being. The nature of his father's job as a police officer led to frequent relocations, exposing Alimamy to the unique and diverse cultural experiences of Sierra Leone. While enriching, these experiences also deprived him of the chance to adapt to his traditional Kono culture.

Resilience became Alimamy's lifeline amidst overwhelming misfortunes. On Tuesday, 11th May 1964, his life took a dramatic turn, instilling in him a profound love and fear of God. That day, during a routine transfer for his father's job, the family set out on a journey that ended in tragedy, leaving Alimamy as the sole survivor of a devastating road accident.

Hospitalized at Bo Government Hospital, Alimamy was adopted by Ms. Ann Marie, the compassionate matron. After a year, she enrolled him in Bo Comprehensive Secondary School. When Ms. Ann Marie retired, they moved to Waterloo, where Alimamy continued his education under challenging circumstances.

Despite life's hardships, Alimamy remained determined to pursue his dreams. After the untimely death of Ms. Ann Marie, he had to abandon his studies and become an apprentice, learning the tailoring trade. This skill gave him the means to support himself and achieve his dream of aiding his less privileged compatriots.

Alimamy's life was once again upended by a catastrophic event on 22nd December 1984, which profoundly changed his outlook. From that day forward, he dedicated his life to helping others, founding a philanthropic organization to reduce the number of street children in the country.

ACKNOWLEDGMENTS

Pastor Victor Ajisafe of the Sanctuary Praise Church in Freetown, Sierra Leone, and Pastor Mark Kamara of the Winners Chapel Church, Goderich Branch, Freetown, Sierra Leone, inspired me to write this book. Their consistent preaching of the words of God enlightened me and inspired me to change my lifestyle. More than many years ago, I began writing poems, lyrics, and scripts but never dared to tap into them more seriously. Their sermons enabled me to unlock my potential.

After attending a particular service at the Sanctuary Church during one of its "Let My Gate Be Opened" sessions in late 2014, I felt Pastor Ajisafe was speaking directly to me. His sermon was titled "Making Use of Your Talent. " In it, he referred to the "Parable of the Talents," which talks of a master and his servants.

The parable begins when the master leaves his house to travel. Before leaving, the master entrusts his property to his servants according to each person's abilities. The property entrusted to the three servants was worth eight talents, where talent was a significant amount of money. The first servant received five talents, the second received two talents, and the third received one talent. Upon returning home after a long absence, the master asked his three servants to account for their stewardship. The first and second servants explained that they each put their talents to work and doubled the value of the property they were entrusted with. The master told them, "Well done, you are good and faithful servants."

The third servant, however, had merely hidden his talent. He had buried it in the ground and was punished by his master for laziness and not using his talent well. At that point, I began to see myself in the place of the third servant, who did not use his talent well. As a result, I started writing this story but stopped halfway after real-izing my writing was not immediately rewarding.

While putting this work together, many people contributed significantly in diverse ways. I sincerely thank Dr. Joe Ben Davies, Ambassador Alhaji Brima E. Koroma, Ibrahim K. Koroma, and my wife Francess, daughter Edna, for their careful perusal of the entire manuscript and their comments, which helped shape the final work immensely. I also thank my family for their encouragement, especially my wife, Mrs. Francess Gbonda-Fode, and my daughter, Edna Ahfuma Tucker, who inspired me in my writing career. I was unemployed when I started writing this book, but Edna always said, "Daddy, you are fully employed without salary; payment will soon come after you have completed your book." Those words were encouraging and challenging, keeping me zealous to complete this book.

ABOUT THE AUTHOR

Mr. Sonny Anthony Tucker was born on 22nd November 1962 to Mr. and Mrs. Jolly Tucker.

He is the fourth born of ten children. He is married to Mrs. Francess Kadie Gbonda-Fode and has four children, including his two biological children, Sonia Barbie Tucker and Edna Ahfuma Tucker. He attained his primary education at Samaria Primary School in Freetown. Upon completion, he enrolled at the Government Model Secondary School in Freetown, Sierra Leone, where he sat for the West African General Certificate Examination.

In 1982, he moved to Liberia to join his elder sister Cecilia and further his education. He was enrolled at Samuel Ford Dennis High School, where he completed his secondary education. Upon graduation, he attended the City Commercial Institute, earning a diploma that certified him as a Junior Accountant. He graduated from the University of Liberia in December 1996 with a Bachelor's degree in Business Administration with an emphasis on accounting. By profession, he is an accountant.

During the height of the civil war in Liberia in 1995, he worked as an Admin Officer to the Shipping Manager for Pacific Architecture and Engineering (PAE), a Lockheed Martin Company. PAE provided logistical support to the Economic Community of West African States Monitoring Group (ECOMOG).

Due to the intensity of the civil war and the destruction of the airport in Liberia, Sonny was transferred to PAE Sierra Leone. He coordinated with authorities at the US Embassy in Freetown, Sierra Leone, and the Government of Sierra Leone to grant permission to land C-21 United States Military Cargo Flights, providing logistical support for Liberia's peacekeeping force.

He worked for PAE for over thirteen years in various capacities: Administrative Assistant, Ground Air Operator Assistant, Supervisor of Fuel Station and Lead Expediter, and Assistant Procurement Manager. Sonny was also sent to the Republic of Chad, where he joined the PAE Chad Team and worked for ten months as a Supply Administrative Officer.

Upon returning to Sierra Leone, he continued his service with PAE until February 2011. On May 6th, 2011, he joined African Felix Juice Factory as Supply Chain Manager, where he worked for almost four years before getting involved in his family business owned by his elder sister Cecilia.

On 29th January 2023, Sonny moved to London, United Kingdom, where he now works and lives with his wife.

CHAPTER ONE
LIFE IN FREETOWN

Alimamy Bangalie came from a humble background. His parents had migrated from the Eastern part of Sierra Leone to the capital city, Freetown, in search of a better livelihood. Both parents were of Kono tribe descent, which made their union easy. Alimamy's father, Ibrahim Bangalie, was fortunate to be recruited by the Sierra Leone Police, where he met Ami Fallah, a trader selling fruits and vegetables for her elder sister.

Despite Alimamy's father being a police officer, most community members did not know the family. They isolated themselves to the extent that they were never members of any social or religious body. Alimamy and his siblings were left to decide what course to take in spiritual or religious matters. At one point, he and his two elder sisters started their lives without understanding the relevance of being religious but were captivated when they saw their friends attending religious functions. As time went by, life became more interesting, and they began assimilating with some Christian friends in their neighborhood, especially on Good Friday, Easter Sunday, and Christmas. They were privileged to join their friends on beach trips during those festivals, encouraging them to follow Christian beliefs and doctrines.

Contrarily, their father, who had always professed to be a Muslim but had never practiced any Islamic dogmas or been seen at the Masjid despite its closeness to their residence, preferred his children to be Muslims. At age nine, Alimamy's interest in Christianity grew tremendously. Fortunately for him, a church in his community called Angel of Christ Ministry, a Pentecostal Church headed by Pastor Alphonso Browne, became a place of involvement for him in most church activities. Prayer and fasting were not unique to him; sometimes, he pretended to fast to cover the lack of food at home. With God's intervention, he and his family overcame abject poverty when his mother started trading in a communal market close to their home called Congo Market.

At age ten, Alimamy started school at Saint Edwards Primary, a Catholic missionary school located at Ford Street. The mission was benevolent, providing uniforms, books, and daily meals for their pupils to encourage children like Alimamy to be punctual at school. The school compound was fenced, preventing pupils from leaving school unnoticed. It was a two-story building with over eighteen classrooms from kindergarten to Class seven, excluding the Head Teacher's office and the staff room. The school had a large compound for recreational activities and a playground where most social and sporting activities were held. The toilet facilities were good, and Alimamy would often use one before going home each day because the toilet at home was in poor condition. St. Edwards School's environment and facilities were quite impressive.

There were many academic and athletic activities in school, which he enjoyed very much, and he was among the best pupils in his class. His best subject was Mathematics, and by Class Two, he had memorized the Multiplication Table from levels one to twelve. He needed to improve in Arts and Crafts, which he did not enjoy, but he came second in being promoted to Class Three. Being the oldest in his class, most of his friends about his age were in higher classes.

The janitors regularly cleaned the school compound, classrooms, and toilets, but pupils were sometimes made to clean the bathrooms or recreational facilities when they misbehaved as part of their / punishment. A school nurse administered first-aid treatment to pupils suffering from minor illnesses. Usually, pupils were placed in the observation room for a few minutes to ensure their condition improved and then sent back to class. For severe cases, the nurse referred pupils to the government hospital downtown. Later, the head teacher would send the school messenger to the pupil's parents to inform them about their child's health status or contact them via telephone for those privileged to have home phones.

At one stage, Alimamy was infected with cholera in Class Three without his parent's knowledge. In October 1964, after devotion, he suffered severe stomach pain leading to an involuntary bowel movement, which left visible stains on his blue khaki shorts. Embarrassed, he quickly ran to the toilet to clean up, but while taking off his shorts, the bowel movement intensified, followed by vomiting. Fortunately, one of the school janitors was cleaning a nearby toilet when she heard someone vomiting and quickly ran to his aid. Despite her efforts, the vomiting continued, followed by more involuntary bowel movements. She hastily ran to the school's first aid nurse and explained his condition.

The nurse, an experienced professional in service for almost twenty-five years, knew precisely what action to take for Alimamy's health. Both women, being mothers, were empathetic to his condition and understood the severe consequences of cholera if not treated promptly.

They rushed to the toilet, where they found Alimamy lying on the floor, pale and weak. The nurse administered some treatment, and the janitor cleaned him up and took him to the clinic. There, the nurse checked his pulse and temperature.

While under observation, Alimamy's condition worsened, and he began vomiting again with more involuntary bowel movements. He became weak and unable to move, prompting an urgent transfer to Connaught Hospital, where many people were suffering from cholera. Despite its designation, Connaught, the premier state hospital, lacked significant facilities and resources to respond to various illnesses. Facilities such as electricity and water, the lifeblood of any medical center, were poor, making patients' conditions precarious. The hospital was highly congested with cholera patients, and measures to combat the disease were inadequate.

The hospital beds were in poor condition, and when Alimamy was ushered into one of the wards by a nurse, he was laid on an old, deplorable bed, but he had no choice. Another nurse, probably of senior rank, approached the bed holding a bottle of oral rehydration salts (ORS) and told him to down it. He was also given intravenous fluids with antibiotics.

On another bed, a few meters away, a young boy

between the ages of three and five years battled for his life until he slowly succumbed to the dreadful cholera disease in his mother's lap. Earlier, the young boy had been rushed to the hospital, but his condition deteriorated rapidly, and all efforts by the nurses to save his life were in vain. The dead boy's mother screamed in anguish, pressing her entire body on her dead child, and the whole ward erupted into pandemonium. It was a painful moment watching two porters take the remains of her son, which she did not want to relinquish.

Coincidentally, Alimamy's parents were about to enter the hospital when they heard the cries of a woman who had lost her child. They rushed into the ward to check on their son's condition and found Alimamy lying in bed, being monitored by a nurse while receiving the last bottle of drip. At about 5:30 pm, he was discharged and went home with his parents.

They found one of their neighbor's houses crammed with people on arrival. Some were crying, and others looked sad. Alimamy's father went to inquire what had happened and was met at the entrance by a neighbor, Mr. Momoh, who told him the tragic news. Yeanor, the daughter of another neighbor, Mr. Saidu Turay, had succumbed to cholera. She had frequent stools and vomiting early in the morning, but her parents did not take her to the hospital on time, and she passed away.

On hearing the news of Yeanor's death, Alimamy was shocked. The previous evening, they had all been playing a local game, "Ardie" around the water well where they had fetched water. The memory of Yeanor, so full of life, now gone, haunted him. Earlier that day, two other people in the community were rushed to the hospital in severe condition, but fortunately, they survived. The community was gripped with fear as the cholera epidemic raged across the country, claiming the lives of many.

On the following Sunday, the church service saw fewer attendees. The pews, once filled with familiar faces, now seemed eerily empty, a stark reminder of those who were either ill or had died from the dreadful cholera. Alimamy, trembling with fear and gratitude, gave testimony in church, thanking God for saving him from the same fate that had claimed Yeanor. His voice wavered, and tears welled up in his eyes as he spoke, the weight of his survival bearing heavily on his young shoulders.

Alimamy and his family resided at number 7 Morgan Lane, Brookfields, a community of people from different ethnic backgrounds living in a congested environment. Krio was the predominant language widely spoken in the community, but the Limba tribe, known for their cultural manifestations, was in the majority. Their celebrations often involved gatherings along the streets with people in masquerades called "Matorma." Paradoxically, Alimamy was always afraid of the Matorma, even though he was curious to see it performing.

A chronic water supply problem forced many people to use the local stream within Brookfields and the surrounding communities. On Saturdays, Alimamy and his siblings would walk about ten minutes to the stream, which had become a water reservoir for washing and laundering. It was also a meeting point for boys and girls wishing to see friends away from their homes. Throughout the day, the presence of people around the stream was strong, and it became even more robust during the weekends.

Most of the time, Alimamy and his siblings would go to the stream because the water was clean. After washing their clothes, they sometimes swam in the stream or climbed nearby trees to pick fruits. Some trees were tall and risky to climb as the branches could easily break. Therefore, they would sometimes throw stones at the fruits, occasionally hitting people or damaging the roofs of buildings. This behavior upset the residents, leading them to cut down the trees, inadvertently undermining the sustainability of the streams.

At an early age, Alimamy's mother introduced him to selling kerosene in his community. The proceeds each day were used for the family's upkeep. Each evening, excluding Sundays, he would sell before going to church. After school, late in the afternoons, he and his elder sister, Hawa, would go to the BP Filling Station at St. John and purchase a gallon of kerosene for three Leones.

In the evenings, he would take his container of kerosene and three different-sized measuring bottles and go out to sell. He established excellent relationships with many older women in the community who patronized him as he sold kerosene. They were fond of him and called him all sorts of nicknames, such as "my husband," "Mr. Handsome," and "my boy lollipop." Sometimes, these women even gave him money for lunch when they saw him.

Selling kerosene became one of Alimamy's joyful moments, a brief respite from the harsh realities of life. He would always finish selling early, then join his friends to play football in the quieter part of one of the streets if he was lucky to be selected for a team. These moments of play were precious, offering him a fleeting sense of normalcy and happiness amidst the ever-looming threats of illness and poverty.

Alimamy's life was a tapestry of survival and fleeting joys woven with threads of hardship and resilience. His experiences, though filled with sorrow and struggle, shaped the person he was becoming. Each day was a battle and a testament to the enduring human spirit, finding light in the darkest times.

Before heading to the playground, Alimamy always ensured he securely pocketed the money from his kerosene sales. This was his safeguard against misplacing it. Sometimes, he'd linger with the kids or grandchildren of the women who bought his kerosene, discussing their school lessons and receiving their admiration. Despite coming from a low-income family, Alimamy was content with his modest means, and to his surprise, many of his friends envied him. His handsome features and fair complexion often drew admiration, though it remained unclear if this played a role in the women's fondness for him.

One day, as Alimamy set out to sell kerosene, he encountered a man standing by an old Volkswagen that looked abandoned. The man said, "Young man, what are you selling?" Alimamy replied, "Kerosene." The man's soft, reassuring voice continued, "Oh my God, that's good. I wish I had a son who could sell kerosene for me." He touched Alimamy's shoulder with a warm smile and handed him two coins. "This is for you; this other one is for you to buy me two sticks of Hollywood cigarettes from that shop over there."

Feeling a surge of trust, Alimamy left his gallon of kerosene and measuring bottles with the man and ran to the shop. When he asked for the cigarettes, he was met with questions he didn't understand: "Which brand? Filler or menthol?" Alimamy, unfamiliar with cigarettes, chose "Menthol." Seeing the boy's confusion, the shopkeeper returned his money and instructed him to ask the person for the specific brand.

On his way back, he bought five sweets using the money the stranger gave him. He unwrapped one and began to suck on it, finding brief comfort in the sweet taste. But when he returned to the old Volkswagen, the man was gone with the gallon of Kerosine, leaving his three measuring bottles in the car. Panic gripped him as he searched the area, but the man had vanished. Alimamy, disheartened and tearful, wandered the neighborhood, his thoughts consumed by the trouble he'd faced at home. He feared the inevitable scolding from his mother, but what troubled him most was the prospect of disappointing her.

Desperate, he turned to some of his regular customers for help. His journey led him to Mrs. Duncan's house. Mrs. Duncan, a widow with no children, had once asked Alimamy's mother if she could adopt him. Mama Ami had refused, as Alimamy was her only son. As he approached

Mrs. Duncan, he noticed she was returning from a funeral.

Upon seeing him, Mrs. Duncan called out concernedly, "My husband! My husband! Why are you crying? What's wrong?" As Alimamy began to explain, she took his arm and guided him up the front steps of her home. Unlocking the door with a set of keys, she ushered him into a small but cozy living room. This was the first time he'd been inside her house, having always met her in the backyard where he sold kerosene.

Mrs. Duncan listened intently as Alimamy recounted his ordeal. Her eyes filled with empathy as she handed him a generous amount of money, instructing him to be cautious of strangers. She brought him a slice of banana cake and a soft drink bottle. As he ate, she advised him to be careful and wary of people who might deceive him. Since then, Mrs. Duncan always kept something for him —biscuits, cakes, donuts, or rice bread.

Alimamy eagerly left, cherishing her kindness. Though he went home without the gallon of kerosene and no profit for the day, he felt a sense of relief. When he arrived home, he shared the incident with his mother and sisters, but they were skeptical, assuming he had lost some kerosene while playing football. Despite his attempts to explain, they remained unconvinced. The encounter with the stranger had taught Alimamy a lesson he would never forget.

The next day, as he passed through the area where he'd been duped, he hoped to catch sight of the thief but found no trace of him.

On February 17th, 1965, Alimamy's father received a transfer letter moving the family from Freetown to Matotoka. Alimamy was thrilled, envisioning a new and improved life, especially since they would be moving into a police barracks. However, his friends and teacher were saddened by the news, having grown fond of him through his active participation in community activities. Pastor Brown had even wanted Alimamy to stay with him at the parsonage, but Mama Ami had declined the offer.

When Alimamy shared the news with Mrs. Duncan, she was visibly distressed and saw it as an opportune moment to renew her request to adopt him. That evening, after selling kerosene to Mrs. Duncan, she asked him to visit her after he finished his rounds. He promptly went to her house, where she sat alone on the veranda, engrossed in the Bible. Her face lit up upon seeing him, and she welcomed him with a warm embrace.

As they sat together, she spoke about her renewed intention to adopt him, believing it would be more practical for Alimamy to continue his education in Freetown rather than move to the province. Alimamy was preoccupied with their upcoming relocation and shared details about their new apartment and the motorbike that would take him and his siblings to school. Mrs. Duncan listened, her smile unwavering despite her concern.

Upon arriving at Alimamy's house, Mrs. Duncan approached his mother, who was sitting at the entrance. She greeted her and made her request known. Surprised and irritated by the late visit, Mama Ami shouted, "Madam, I have told you several times that I cannot give my son to anyone. Please, look elsewhere if you are so desperate for a child." The exchange was tense, leaving Mrs. Duncan in silent distress. She stood for a moment, tears streaming down her face, before wishing Alimamy farewell with a heartfelt prayer, struggling to regain her composure before leaving.

CHAPTER TWO

TRANSFER TO NORTHERN PROVINCE

On January 3rd, 1953, Alimamy and his family embarked on their journey from the bustling streets of Freetown to the quiet, remote village of Matotoka, located about seventeen miles from Magburaka, the administrative heart of Tonkolili District in Sierra Leone's Northern Province. As the old truck rumbled over the rugged terrain, Alimamy's anticipation for a fresh start was soon overshadowed by the stark reality of his new home. The vibrant lights of Freetown were replaced by an oppressive darkness, punctuated only by the distant croaking of frogs and the chirping of crickets.

The moment they arrived, Alimamy's excitement deflated. The absence of pipe-borne water, electricity, and well-paved roads contrasted sharply with the conveniences he had left behind. The dusty, uneven paths and the shadowy silhouettes of palm trees added to his sense of isolation. Tears welled up in his eyes as he thought of Mrs. Duncan, whose offer of adoption now seemed like a missed opportunity for a better life. He lay down in the cramped room he shared with his sisters, the room's thin walls offering little comfort as he pondered how he might persuade his mother to reconsider Mrs. Duncan's offer.

Though television was a luxury to his family, Alimamy had been able to watch films at the homes of neighboring friends. Matotoka, however, had only one primary school, the Roman Catholic School, where he was placed in Class Four. The quality of education here was dishearteningly poor compared to St. Edwards. Teachers were notorious for their sporadic attendance and meager dedication, often neglecting their duties to tend to their farms. It was common for pupils to be pulled from school to assist in agricultural work, including weeding and harvesting.

Alimamy's initial days in Matotoka were marked by loneliness and frustration. The Themne language was a significant barrier, leaving him isolated from his peers. However, driven by his determination to fit in, he diligently practiced Themne, overcoming laughter from local children at his early mistakes. His persistence paid off as he quickly became proficient, mastering the language before his sisters.

Tragedy struck when Alimamy fell ill with dysentery, a result of the polluted stream that served as the village's primary water source. The stream, often tainted with human waste and other contaminants, was a health hazard. Alimamy endured excruciating abdominal pain, fever, and shivering. The local healer's treatments provided temporary relief but failed to address the worsening symptoms. The situation escalated, leading to severe vomiting and bloody diarrhea.

His mother sought help from the Magburaka medical clinic, far from Matotoka. Magburaka, bustling with activity compared to the tranquility of Matotoka, offered a stark contrast to his former village. Alimamy spent two nights in the clinic, his anxiety about medical examinations amplified by memories of his friend Ishmael, who had succumbed to injuries at the same facility. Seeing an old, rusty X-ray machine in the corner of the room only heightened his fears.

The clinic's staff, including a weary nurse with a stern demeanor, conducted a physical examination. Despite the discomfort, Alimamy's condition required urgent attention, and he was placed on a saline drip with a combination of antibiotics and anti-amoebic medications. The treatment was costly, depleting the last of his mother's savings. Sergeant Bangalie, Alimamy's father, arrived later, eliciting a heated argument with Mama Ami, who was frustrated by his absence during their son's illness. Sergeant Bangalie's lack of involvement in family matters only exacerbated her distress.

In Matotoka, agriculture became Alimamy's new focus. Unlike the busy academic life in Freetown, he engaged in farming activities and participated in communal labor, which was a cornerstone of village life. He joined his peers in cultivating vegetable gardens, setting traps for rodents, and participating in community workdays, where farm owners provided food and hired "Praise Singers" to boost morale.

The cultural fabric of Matotoka was rich with traditions. During the dry season, cultural events flourished, including dances and storytelling sessions under the full moon. The local storyteller, Pa Aruna, captivated audiences with tales like "Treat Your Secret – Secret." The story, about a revered hunter betrayed by a jealous rival, imparted lessons on trust and secrecy, engaging Alimamy and his friends.

In December and January, the village buzzed with the rice harvest and the initiation of young girls into the Bondo Society, marking their transition into womanhood. Alimamy's sisters faced social pressure as they had not yet undergone initiation. Eager to avoid scandal, Mama

Ami sought to enroll them despite the financial strain. The ceremony in Matotoka involved elaborate rituals and public celebrations, including parading through the village's dusty roads, singing songs to ascertain that they had completed the symbol of womanhood, and then converging at the Courthouse. Alimamy was perplexed by the spectacle of older men vying to marry these girls, a practice that seemed at odds with his understanding of social norms.

Interestingly, priority was given to the Paramount Chief and his cohorts to choose the girl they wished to marry before the commoners. On that occasion, Paramount Chief Bai Kandeh the Third was in his late eighties with seven wives and did not attend due to ill health. Several men came out wanting to pay the bride price for Alimamy's two sisters. Still, their mother rejected their offers, telling them she had already received bride prices for her daughters and would not want to complicate issues. She only said that because she wanted her daughters to continue their education rather than get married at a young age.

As Alimamy approached Class Seven, the crucial year for the Common Entrance Examination, his hopes of returning to Freetown seemed to hinge on his performance. The transfer to Bo Town, however, quashed his dreams. Bo Town, a lively second capital with features reminiscent of Freetown, promised new opportunities but brought new challenges. Alimamy's father had enrolled him in a local school. Despite his longing for Freetown, Alimamy faced the reality of another transition, leaving behind the world he had begun to make his own in Matotoka.

CHAPTER THREE
EXPERIENCE IN THE SOUTHERN PROVINCE

As the torrential rain pounded relentlessly, Alimamy, his sisters, and his parents set out for Bo Town, their journey marked by the storm's fury. The driver, a maestro of the road, maneuvered through the deluge and the treacherous potholes with an almost supernatural skill. Their arrival at Bo was nothing short of a miracle. The sight of the Bo Police Barracks, with its well-lit streets and reliable pipe-borne water, was a beacon of hope amidst the storm.

The Barracks were an intricate maze of forty-one buildings, each block inscribed with BR – BLOCK, followed by a unique identifier. The Bangalie family was assigned to BR - Block F-3. Few were designated for senior officers among the structures, while others housed the low-ranking officers. The Barracks boasted a Church, a

Mosque, a primary school, and a modest clinic. Only senior officers' quarters had self-contained toilets, whilst lower-rank officers shared toilet facilities scattered at the barracks' four cardinal points. The toilets, though sufficient, were crowded, making early mornings a race for privacy. The bustling market at the east end of the barracks became a lifeline for Alimamy's mother, who eagerly participated as a trader.

Bo Town, though vibrant, lacked the grandeur of Freetown. It lacked government prestige, its streets were less paved, and its buildings shorter. Alimamy was admitted to Form 1A at Ahmadiyya Muslim Secondary School Bo. His friendship with Kelfala Gbondo, who performed poorly and was often truant from school, was seen at Coronation Field, riding bicycles, playing football, or gambling, which Alimamy had found pleasure faced an uphill battle in his education.

Indeed, his previous schooling in Matotoka had yet to prepare him for Ahmadiyya's rigorous standards. His initial examinations were disastrous, revealing a stark contrast between his past achievements and his current dismal performance.

Classes became a grind, and Alimamy often found himself drifting into sleep. The school's Principal, Mr. Lahai, summoned him to his office, coinciding with disciplinary action from his English teacher, Mrs. Kaikai. As Alimamy sat in the principal's spacious office, the gravity of his academic failings loomed large. Mr. Lahai's stern gaze and probing questions unearthed an unexpected revelation: Alimamy's report card from his previous school was filled with high marks, a stark contrast to his current underperformance. Suspicion lingered—was his father's influence a factor in his past successes?

Mr. Lahai's words were a harsh wake-up call. The principal's threat of expulsion and his disappointment in Alimamy's lackluster performance were chilling. The fear of being expelled was a harsh reality check, igniting a fierce determination within Alimamy. His struggle was not just academic but deeply personal; he grappled with distractions and a lack of supervision.

The pressures at home were formidable. His eldest sister, Hawa, who was supposed to help him with his studies, was extremely busy after school, constantly engaged in domestic work, and would join her mother to sell in the market. His other sister Bendu, who was only two years older than him, couldn't help either, as she had problems with her studies, and his father, Sergeant Bangalie, was rarely present. When he did come home, his presence was often marked by drunken disputes with their mother.

Despite being illiterate, Ma Ami was unwavering in her dedication to her children's education. Her sacrifices were evident in her relentless efforts to support their schooling. She sometimes took time off her busy schedule to visit her children at their schools and talk with their teachers to ascertain their performances and punctuality.

During one of her visits to Alimamy's school, one of his teachers told her that Alimamy was not there. The pain in Ma Ami's eyes upon learning of Alimamy's truancy was a powerful catalyst for change. She became worried, thinking something might have gone wrong with her son. Immediately, she went to the police station to tell her husband about the unfortunate event. Upon her arrival, she was told that her husband had gone on an assignment. She did not explain to anyone; instead, she went home expecting to meet Alimamy, but to no avail.

Alimamy got home at the usual time, pretending to be from school. He greeted his mother, but she did not respond or receive him as expected, and couldn't comprehend the cause of her change. She was angry but decided to be patient and allowed him to change his uniform and eat his food, and then she would confront him.

Later, she took him into her bedroom and explained what she learned at his school. She cried while talking, which caused Alimamy to cry too. Alimamy's resolve solidified after a heart-wrenching conversation with his mother. Her tears and his subsequent promise to strive for excellence marked a turning point. He vowed to honor her sacrifices and make her proud, a commitment that shaped his future.

A new friendship with Brima Rogers, a top student from a wealthy family, brought a transformative influence into Alimamy's life. Brima's generosity, motivational insights, and shared study sessions dramatically improved Alimamy's academic performance. The joy of his second-term results was a testament to his newfound focus and hard work. His family's celebration of his achievements underscored the profound impact of his dedication.

The third term's examinations were a crucible of challenge and opportunity. Alimamy, driven by his past experiences and Brima's motivational quotes, achieved a commendable fifth place in his class. Upon receiving his report card, he immediately went to his Principal's office; unfortunately, he was not there. He then went home with a heart full of joy and excitement to tell her mother and the rest of the family the good news.

When he arrived home, he gave the report card to his mother, who gently handed it to his elder sister, Hawa. She opened it and began explaining his performance. You could sense the joy and happiness of his family. Ma Ami held her son closer to herself and later placed him on her back, dancing in their living room. They all rejoice.

His success was celebrated with new school supplies and the joy of familial pride. Ma Ami's resourcefulness, despite limited means, was a testament to her boundless love and support. She bought him some new clothes, a pair of shoes, three sets of uniforms, two pairs of trainers, all of his school books, and an Adidas football. He was surprised to receive the items because he knew how difficult it would have been for his mother to provide them.

Alimamy asks his mother, "Mama Ami, where did you get the money to purchase all these items?" She gave him a warm smile and said, "It's through the Grace of God." He smiled at her and replied, "Amen". After a couple of seconds, while inspecting the items, he asked her again but paraphrased his question. "Mama Ami, whoever gave you that money must have been very generous." She then said, "Oh my son, Alimamy, you are always curious to know things," but she was interrupted by Alimamy, who said, "Mama, it's not that I am curious; it's just because I want to know so that I can express my thanks and appreciation to that person."

There was a bit of silence in the room. She replied honestly, "Yes, you are right, my dear son. " She paused, looking at him in his eyes, and said, "I got the money from our local saving scheme, Osusu, at the market." He interrupted her again and said, "Wow. Will you repay huge money to the Market, Osusu?"

"No, no, my son, I am not going to pay a cent," she lied/ or added. He then asked, "What do you mean, Mama?" She replied, "Now listen, since I saw your second term report card, you made me happy, and I thought it wise to respond by saving some money to buy your school needs." There was complete silence in the room, and tears ran down his eyes. Unexpectedly, she quietly left him in his small room. In her absence, he began meditating on reciprocating and supporting his mother when he should have grown up, which played in his mind until he fell asleep.

It was during this period that he began playing football seriously. Before now, he could hardly be selected for any of the teams because he was not skillful enough, but by having his football, he was always selected, which helped improve his skills.

Sometimes, he joined Brima and his brothers in watching movies and concerts at Opera Cinema Hall. Despite having fun with his colleagues during the vacation, he had always found time to read his books. He was convinced that only through education could he be in a favorable position to help his mother out of her predicament, as she had placed most of her resources on his education, which he highly cherished.

On the first day, when school resumed for another academic school year, Alimamy's Principal took him to his office after devotion and gave him two short story books with two pounds (£2.00) cash to show his appreciation and to encourage him to excel. He was delighted to be able to fulfill his promise. Alimamy felt high in spirit, knowing that the accomplishment of a man rests solely in his hands and, of course, Brima Rogers's proverb reflected in his mind. He could have been a drop-out like Kelfala, who stopped attending school long before they sat for their second term examination.

Yet, a new upheaval loomed just as Alimamy was finding his footing. His father's transfer to Koindu disrupted his burgeoning life in Bo. Torn between his attachment to Bo and the persuasive pleas of his sister Hawa, Alimamy faced the uncertainty of relocation, bracing himself for yet another chapter in his tumultuous journey.

In the ebb and flow of his experiences, Alimamy's determination to rise above his circumstances became his beacon, guiding him through the trials and triumphs of his youthful years.

CHAPTER FOUR

TRANSFER TO EASTERN PROVINCE

With its rugged beauty and untamed spirit, the eastern region of Sierra Leone held the small town of Koindu in its grasp. Nestled in the Kailahun District and flanked by the borders of Liberia and Guinea, Koindu was a world apart from Bo's bustling, modern city. Unlike Bo, it lacked the conveniences of pipe-borne water, electricity, and paved roads. Yet, it brimmed with vibrant commercial life—a unique culture.

Alimamy and his family had just relocated to this vibrant yet starkly different environment. The Bangalie family adapted swiftly because Mende was also the local language at Koindu, thanks to their previous stay in Bo, where Mende was also the local dialect. Koindu, despite its modest infrastructure, was a hub of commerce, drawing merchants from across West Africa. Its streets were alive with the hum of trade, its markets bursting with rare commodities not found elsewhere in Sierra Leone.

Alimamy was enrolled in the Koindu Agricultural Secondary School (KASS), a modest institution with only eight teachers, including the principal, Mr. Vandy, who taught English and literature. Alimamy's presence was magnetic. He quickly became a favorite of Mr. Vandy, known for his eloquence and intellect, a testament to his education at Ahmadiyya Secondary School in Bo. At KASS, Alimamy was in Form 2 among a diverse group of students, including eight Liberians and five Guineans. The Liberians, with their warmth and affluence, particularly appealed to Alimamy, who found himself drawn into their circle.

While Alimamy's academic prowess earned him respect and admiration, his personal life was equally tumultuous. His preference for boys over girls did little to quell the attention of female classmates, who showered him with gifts to win his favor. Alimamy, ever the tactician, played along, feigning curiosity while relishing the perks.

Among these admirers was Satta Konneh, a striking Liberian girl with a fair complexion and a height that made her presence commanding. Her affection for

Alimamy was evident; she would bring him lunch daily, and the two often spent time together. Yet, despite their closeness, Alimamy was determined to keep their relationship platonic, insisting they wait until after senior high school. This stance frequently ignited Satta's fiery temper, leading to dramatic confrontations.

Another significant figure in Alimamy's life was Sia Fayiah, the daughter of the Paramount Chief. Beautiful and generous, Sia's interest in Alimamy was marked by her frequent gifts and a poetic love letter. The competition for Alimamy's affection reached a fever pitch during the School Inter-House Sports event, where Satta and Sia's rivalry erupted into a fierce brawl.

The event was a spectacle of athletic prowess and emotional turmoil. Alimamy excelled, winning races and contributing to his house's impressive performance. Satta cheered fervently for Alimamy, her support becoming jealous as Sia congratulated him with a peck on the cheek. The confrontation that followed was explosive. Satta, fueled by rage, slapped Sia, igniting a brutal fight that left both girls bruised and humiliated. Alimamy, stunned and unable to intervene, watched as the two girls were dragged apart.

The fallout from the fight was severe. Satta's fury over Alimamy's perceived lack of support strained their relationship. She was dismayed when Alimamy suggested she address him directly about her concerns rather than resorting to violence. Their argument lingered, clouded by her insistence on protecting their relationship through conflict.

As Alimamy had been one of its best students, who participated in almost all the school activities, including quizzes, sports, and games, he was expected to play in the football match between his school, KASS, and a school from the Liberian side of the border called Voinjama High School (VHS). Many spectators converged at the field to watch that game, which commenced at 4:00 pm.

The first half of the match ended goalless. Even though KASS had dominated, they could not score, thanks to the brilliant display by the Voinjama (VHS) goalkeeper. When they resumed for the second forty-five minutes, KASS was still on top, and Alimamy was all over the field being marked by two players from the VHS; in the eighty-fifth minute, Alimamy was fouled inside the penalty box by one of VHS's defenders after he dribbled the ball around and skillfully passed the ball between his legs. The referee immediately blew his whistle and pointed to the penalty spot.

Alimamy was chosen to take the spot kick, which he took with great aplomb as he sent the keeper the wrong way and scored the goal. The crowd went wild with shouting, singing, and dancing. Even his father, who never showed any interest in his children's schooling, was amongst the jubilant crowd and beaming with evident pride in his son. Alimamy's performance in the match only increased his popularity at Koindu and across the border to Liberia. Had it not been for the brilliant performance of the VHS Goalkeeper, KASS would have scored not less than four goals.

After that match, Alimamy's popularity spread like wildfire. He began receiving letters from older girls who were his seniors proposing a relationship. On one occasion, a girl named Isha gave a letter to Bendu to deliver to Alimamy; instead, she shared the letter with Satta, who later quarreled with Isha. Indeed, most of the girls were resentful of Satta because she was always bragging about Alimamy.

There was another incident between Satta and another girl called Betty Bonner for Alimamy. Betty was the daughter of one of the prominent businessmen in Koindu, whom they nicknamed "Koindu Tycoon." As he and Satta were going through another difficult patch in their relationship, he decided to seize the opportunity to be with Betty, who appeared to have been waiting for such a chance. She had been lavishing money on Alimamy to capture his heart.

At one of the school dances, Satta was already in the hall but refused to dance with any of Alimamy's friends. She was upset that Alimamy had not reached her so that they could come to the dance together. Meanwhile, there were rumors, mostly from Betty's friends, that Alimamy and Satta were no longer friends, as Betty had snatched Alimamy. Even though Alimamy told Betty that he and Satta had some misunderstandings that could be resolved, Betty would not relent in her effort to have an affair with him.

On that night, Alimamy and Betty entered the hall together. The clothes Alimamy wore were bought by Betty, who enjoyed spending her stipend on him. Satta was shocked when she heard Betty's friends yelling, "Mr. and Mrs. Bangalie are on the floor." Satta could not believe her eyes. She ran straight to Alimamy, held him by the collar of his shirt, and began pulling him towards her. Betty stood her ground; she and her friends did not allow Satta to take him away.

During the pushing and shouting, Betty slapped Satta on the face, resulting in a fight. Both of them were brought to the Police Station. Those who went to the police as witnesses testified that Betty was the first to assault Satta. However, being the daughter of Koindu's Tycoon, the police dismissed the case and ordered them to keep the peace. From the police station, Satta hurriedly went to the dance to affirm her presence with Alimamy.

After thirty-two months in Koindu, Alimamy's father had another transfer, this time to Tongo, an area rich in diamonds, in the Kenema District, Eastern Province of Sierra Leone. Their transfer to Tongo not only affected the lives of Alimamy and his family but also had a profound impact on his friends, especially Satta Konneh.

She was utterly devastated when she heard the news of the Bangalie family's transfer from Baindu. She urgently went to Alimamy for confirmation. Her distress was evident as she tearfully confronted Alimamy. She sat on the edge of his bed, her hands on her face, thinking about her future encounters at school and the community. In a minute, she began asking, "So I will lose you! My only friend, my love! Oh my God, where would I be!!! I am going back to Monrovia!!!

Alimamy was surprised but knew Bendu must have told her about their transfer, and he was apprehended for how to relive it for her. He deeply empathized with her, but he could do nothing to remedy the situation. He politely asked her, "Why are you leaving the school?" "I know you are unhappy about my transfer." Satta interrupted him, "I have to return to my father in Monrovia; I can't live here without you being around." There was silence in the room; as he had wanted to coax her, she quickly ran out of his room and went home with a heart full of discomfort.

Although Satta was so angry, a day later, she brought some gifts and two of her most recent photos in appreciation to express her love and to serve as souvenirs in remembrance of their friendship. Before Alimamy could leave Koindu, they took some photos together, but to this day, neither got those photos, as it took days to develop them in that part of the country. Sometimes, photographers go as far as Kenema, some forty-six kilometers from Tongo, to get their photos printed.

Indeed, Satta left Koindu and could not stand the heat and provocation awaiting her after Alimamy's transfer. Early the following morning, she left for Voinjama, the town headquarters of Lofa County, the northern region of Liberia, and subsequently went to Monrovia to continue her schooling.

CHAPTER FIVE

LIFE IN TONGO FIELD

Tongo Field, a town devoid of basic amenities and dependent on diamond mining, starkly contrasts the familiar comforts of Koindu. The town's vibrancy was overshadowed by its economic struggles, making it one of the most expensive places in Sierra Leone.

Alimamy was enrolled at Tongo Field Agriculture Secondary School in Form 4. Like most schools in Sierra Leone, Tongo Field Agricultural Secondary was a co-educational secondary school. It had less than a hundred pipuls, as most of the young boys were engaged in diamond mining. The girls were sent to big towns to further their education due to the escalation of sexual harassment.

Indeed, Alimamy's sister, Hawa, was about five feet eight inches tall, with long black hair, which she always kept in braids. She was aware of her beauty but turned down advances made to her from the opposite sex. After taking the GCE O'Levels examinations at twenty-four, she could not further her education and left to face her trials.

Starting a love affair with Sahr Senesie, a miner, brought familial conflict and ignited a societal scandal. Mama Ami's outrage at Hawa's pre-marital relationship led to a traditional "cleansing" ceremony. This ceremony involved a pledge from the Senesie family asking the Bangalie family forgiveness, bathing of Hawa, payment for sexual assault, slaughtering of a white goat, offering three hundred pieces of white kola nuts, a bag of rice, four bushels of husk rice and five gallons of palm oil to the Bangalie family as compensation.

In acceptance of their pledge, the Bangalie family reciprocated by offering food to the Senesie family and community. On that day, a large crowd witnessed the ceremony. Pa Alhaji Kemokai, a rich and famous diamond dealer, was among the people who went to grace the occasion. There was some merriment with drinks and food to entertain their guests.

During the cleansing ceremony, Pa Alhaji Kemokai set

eyes on Hawa and was determined to have her as his wife. Since that day, he had secretly met Sergeant Bangalie, Hawa's father, and offered him gifts, intending to marry Hawa. Eventually, Sergeant Bangalie accepted his request without consulting his wife or daughter. Mama Ami was furious when she was made aware of the marriage arrangement but had no choice as she had always wanted to be in a healthy and peaceful relationship with her husband.

Although some quarters opposed the marriage between Pa Alhaji Kemokai and Hawa, especially from Pa Kemokai's other wives and extended family members, he was intransigent, and the marriage ceremony arrangements were finalized. Less than a month later, Pa Kemokai and Hawa had their wedding, inviting some of his Lebanese diamond dealer friends, who graced the occasion with many expensive gifts.

A year after their marriage, Hawa delivered a bouncing baby boy, a spitting image of Pa Kemokai. Unfortunately, in less than a week, the baby died from suffocation. The police intervened in the mysterious death of the boy but could not find any culprit, yet fingers were pointed at his other wives, who were always jealous of Hawa.

Due to the influence of Pa Kemokai, who was lavishing money on Hawa's family, Alimamy's lifestyle changed considerably. People began to solicit financial support from him, which triggered his popularity.

He also had the privilege of traveling with Pa Alhaji and his sister Hawa to Freetown to witness the Independence ceremony of Sierra Leone on 27 April 1961 from the British Colonial Master after one hundred fifty years of rule. The occasion was a remarkable and unforgettable event in his life.

Pa Musa Massaquoi, Pa Kemokai's driver, was a tall, light-skinned man who had always been seen chewing kola nuts. He was obedient, faithful, and respectful, ready to carry out Pa Kemokai's errands. He had been working for Pa Kemokai for almost twenty-three years.

On April 25, 1961, they left Tongo for Freetown onboard Pa Kemokai White's Mercedes Benz. Hawa and her husband sat in the back seat while Alimamy sat at the front beside Pa Massaquoi. Alimamy was so excited to reach Freetown after many years. On the way, he began thinking about his classmates and friends, hoping to meet them. One person Alimamy could not stop thinking of was Mrs. Duncan.

They had much fun on their journey to Freetown, and

on arrival, they could notice that something special was about to happen. The streets of Freetown were clean; the sidewalks, zebra crossings, and street light poles were all painted. It was fascinating to observe that most houses on the main streets, from Kissy Ferry Terminal to State House and those from State House to Brookfields Playground, were beautifully painted and decorated. People on the roads celebrated and rejoiced in different ways, singing and dancing as Sierra Leone was to become a sovereign country.

They were booked to stay at the Paramount Hotel, opposite the State House, the Seat of Authority. Alimamy was in room 231, which was excellent and splendid. During those few days, he ate well—steak, lobsters, chicken, and chips. The lives of the Bangalie family changed as they began associating with influential people in their society.

On their return to Tongo, the other wives of Pa Kemokai treated Hawa with malice. They hardly spoke to her and kept throwing hints at her to ignite a quarrel each time their paths crossed.

On their return to Tongo, there was severe animosity between Hawa and the other wives of Pa Kemokai. They became jealous of Hawa, and there were rumors that they were responsible for the death of Hawa's two children, who died prematurely in their infancy.

During this period, Pa Kemokai had just started erecting a house for Hawa at Babadorie in Freetown when he mysteriously died. His sudden death led to suspicion, a series of accusations, and a dramatic funeral. The ensuing chaos saw Pa Kemokai's property and wives redistributed, with Hawa facing hostility from his other wives. His fourth wife, Salamatu, was with him when he complained of stomach aches. Two days before his death, he stopped speaking and vomited a dark color of blood before giving up the ghost.

Upon hearing the death of Pa Kemokai, his wives and some of his daughters went on the rampage, dancing and singing derogatory songs to provoke Hawa. In contrast, others made insulting comments, accusing her of being responsible for the death of their husband and father.

His relatives were not satisfied and called for the service of a Pathologist to conduct an autopsy on his remains. The result showed that someone had poisoned Pa Alhaji, which supported the fact that the body began to decompose quickly and prompted an urgent burial.

During his forty-day ceremony, his brothers took

possession of his property. According to tradition, his brothers could remarry his wives if the wife approved, but only his fourth wife agreed to marry one of the younger brothers. The others, including Hawa, returned to their family homes.

Unfortunately, Hawa and her family lost their claim on the house Pa Alhaji was building for her as she had no document to substantiate ownership. Pa Kemokai's brothers eventually took possession of the unfinished property because Hawa had refused to marry one of the younger brothers, who was also a diamond dealer and had already had three wives.

Hawa went home with a seven-month pregnancy for the late Pa Kemokai, whose brothers were informed about the pregnancy. They promised to assist her with the pregnancy and caring for the baby, but to everyone's surprise, not a cent was sent to Hawa.

Mama Ami, who was careful with money, had invested the money Pa Kemokai and Hawa had given her in a small grocery store and also in a wholesale business, buying drums of palm oil within and around the surrounding villages of Tongo, which she subsequently transported to either Kenema or Bo and sometimes as far as Freetown to sell. After that, she used the money to purchase rice, salt, onion, flour, and Maggi sauce cartons to take to Tongo in exchange for palm oil, which proved highly lucrative.

The mysterious death of Hawa's children and the scandal surrounding Pa Kemokai's death cast a long shadow over Pa Kemokai's wives.

CHAPTER SIX

THE ACCIDENT

At twenty-two, Alimamy had endured four transfers with his family over eight years. Just twenty-one weeks after Hawa had delivered a bouncing baby boy, their father received another telegram for transfer to Gbalamuya Town in the Kambia district, Northern Sierra Leone, along the border with Guinea. Known for its bustling border activities, Gbalamuya hosted a massive presence of security personnel, including Police, Army, Immigration, Customs, and Port Health officers. The government raised significant revenue through customs duties on imported goods from Guinea.

Mama Ami, a dynamic woman, was dedicated to her children's survival and happiness and had always anticipated a transfer. She was unhappy with this one because her thriving business had finally started addressing their economic and social needs, and of course, she had a surplus to save secretly. On the contrary, Alimamy had long been praying for a transfer. His position among his friends had diminished since the death of Pa Kemokai, and he was excited on the day they were leaving Tongo.

He hurriedly dressed and went straight into the old but sturdy police Land Rover sent to transport them to the Tongo car park, where they would board a passenger vehicle to Gbalamuya. As he settled in the car, he heard Hawa shouting, "Alimamy! Alimamy! Where are you?" He replied, "I am in the vehicle." Mama Ami called his name, and Alimamy exited the vehicle to get food. He sluggishly entered the house, where he met his father eating rice with potato leaf soup, sweating profusely. Alimamy ate a small portion, lacking an appetite, but his mum insisted he eat more, which he reluctantly did.

With the driver's help, the family's luggage was loaded into the vehicle, and Alimamy eagerly awaited the journey. However, things moved slower than anticipated. His father suddenly complained of a stomachache and rushed to the toilet, spending an alarmingly long time there. Mama Ami checked on him, and Alimamy tried to listen to their conversation from outside. His father's pain was severe, prompting Mama Ami to send Baindu to fetch a nurse.

After a short while, a male nurse arrived, greeted them softly, and assessed Sergeant Bangalie's condition. He advised postponing the trip, diagnosing low blood pressure, and prescribing medicine. Alimamy felt tears involuntarily streaming down his cheeks, not from concern for his father's health but from the dread of the trip's cancellation and the humiliation he would face from his classmates.

Later, his father's condition improved slightly, and at about 3:30 PM, they decided to proceed to Gbalamuya. Alimamy eagerly woke the driver, Corporal Vandy, and they headed to the vehicle park, where they found only one truck heading to Bo. It had palm oil drums, coffee bags, cacao, and ten other passengers. It was their first time boarding such a vehicle for a transfer, but all Alimamy wanted was to leave Tongo Field.

As they approached Bo, disaster struck. Alimamy's life changed forever, involved in a tragic road accident that claimed the lives of his entire family, including his nephew. Alimamy couldn't remember how it happened; he only remembered waking up in a hospital, bandages wrapped around his head and left arm, pain enveloping his body. He desperately asked for his family, only to be told they had gone home and would visit him later. The nurses, sympathetic to his plight, gave him strong pain relief tablets.

The hospital's Matron, Ms. Ann-Marie Cole, arranged for the police to allow Alimamy to see and identify his family's remains, serving as evidence for the records. On a Sunday morning between 10 AM and 11 AM, three police officers and a medical doctor joined Ms. Ann-Marie to meet Alimamy, who was writing a letter. When asked what he was doing, he replied, "I am writing a letter to my father, asking why he has abandoned me." Their faces showed apprehension, but they remained composed.

Sitting in a chair, Alimamy faced the police officers' interrogation, recounting the names and details of his family. Eventually, the grim truth was revealed: his entire family had perished. The news crushed Alimamy, and when taken to the morgue to identify the bodies, he collapsed, unconscious. Ms. Ann-Marie and Dr. Bernard Thomas resuscitated him and rushed him to the Observation Room.

Lying in his hospital bed, Alimamy's thoughts turned to his bleak future. The kind words of the police officers, urging him to have faith and trust in God, seemed hollow. Alimamy's severe headaches returned, causing him to lose consciousness again, but Ms. Ann-Marie quickly administered medication to put him to sleep.

Weeks passed with no visitors for Alimamy despite repeated announcements by the Sierra Leone Broadcasting Service (SLBS) Radio and Television stations about the fatal accident. Relatives of other survivors visited their loved ones, but Alimamy was alone. The hospital nurses, compassionate and kind, took care of him.

Amidst these challenges, Ms. Ann-Marie Cole decided to adopt Alimamy. Though he was above the typical age for adoption, the Ministry of Social Welfare approved it on September 18, 1966. Proudly announcing herself as Alimamy's new mother, Ms. Ann-Marie bought clothes for his schooling and worked tirelessly to see him happy, especially after losing an academic year in the hospital.

Despite lacking documents to verify his academic status, Ms. Ann-Marie enrolled Alimamy in Form Three at the Bo Comprehensive Secondary. At twenty-three, he was the oldest student, often teased as "Grandpapa" by classmates but remained undeterred. Excelling in his studies, Alimamy's average was an impressive 97.6%, earning high praise from his teachers.

Ms. Ann-Marie's retirement after thirty-two years in nursing dealt another blow to Alimamy's dreams. Her modest pension was insufficient, so they moved to her family home in Waterloo, hoping for a more affordable life. However, life in Waterloo proved challenging. Alimamy noticed people's hostile attitudes towards Ms. Ann-Marie stemming from past grievances.

Despite these difficulties, Alimamy started school at the West Africa Methodist Secondary School (WAM) in Waterloo. Ms. Ann-Marie convinced the principal to allow Alimamy into Form Five due to his excellent performance at his former school, though one teacher, Mrs. Roselyn Williams, opposed it. Determined to make his mother proud, Alimamy worked hard, maintaining top grades despite numerous responsibilities and domestic duties at home.

Ms. Ann-Marie's health deteriorated rapidly, and despite Alimamy's efforts and the village nurse's help, she became bedridden. Alimamy's classmates formed a study group, but he couldn't join due to his caregiving duties. Some female classmates helped with Ms. Ann-Marie's care, bathing and tidying her.

On February 11, 1968, while visiting a friend to copy class notes, Alimamy encountered hostility from an older woman who accused his mother of witchcraft. Shocked and frightened, Alimamy ran home to find his mother shivering with a high fever. Despite his pleas, the village nurse didn't return due to unpaid bills. Desperate, Alimamy sold firewood to support them.

The wood business was fruitful, earning Alimamy respect and the nickname "Mr. Wood." However, those who held grudges against Ms. Ann-Marie never bought from him. On March 18, 1968, during his mock exams, Alimamy learned of Ms. Ann-Marie's death. Though he was expecting her death, her passing was a heavy blow. After the burial, he moved in with his step-sister Susan, facing harsh treatment and overwhelming chores under the control of Mrs. Agnes Smith, Susan's mother-in-law.

Alimamy clung to hope despite the challenges, believing his situation would eventually improve for the better. Friends and teachers, aware of his plight, tried to visit, but Mrs. Smith's hostility often deterred them. Eventually, Alimamy dropped out of school on April 11, 1968, due to financial constraints. He moved in with Mr. and Mrs. Clark, and Mrs. Clark, his former teacher at WAM, offered to pay his fees, but Mr. Clark insisted he learn tailoring.

For seven years, Alimamy apprenticed under Mr. Clark, mastering the skills of a professional tailor while assisting with household chores. Despite the arduous work, Alimamy's dedication earned him Mr. Clark's favor, setting the stage for a future where he could finally carve his life.

CHAPTER SEVEN

MISSION ABROAD

Towards the end of October 1975, Mr. Clarke received a letter from his close friend, Mr. Eddie McDonald, an Englishman he had worked with during their tailoring apprenticeship in the United Kingdom. Mr. McDonald had generously assisted his friend in various ways, and this time, he requested Mr. Clarke to send one of his apprentices to Manchester for advanced tailoring training.

Upon receiving the letter, he went into his inner office, where he relaxed most of the time to have his siesta. After reading the letter for the second time, he called the four apprentices to inform them of the news, which excited them all.

The evening's discussion centered on who would be

the lucky candidate. They agreed that whoever was selected should assist the others financially while living in the United Kingdom. Bobson Jenkins, the eldest apprentice, suggested recommending Alimamy to Mr. Clarke for the trip due to his dedication, hard work, and proficiency in English. However, Fredrick Taylor, the senior apprentice and brother to Mr. Clarke's wife, Melrose, opposed the suggestion, believing it was his opportunity after almost twelve years of service.

Selecting one individual among his four apprentices was tricky for Mr. Clarke. It took him three days to reach a decision. On the third day, Mr. Clarke called a meeting with his apprentices before work, starting with a prayer. This was the first time Mr. Clarke had summoned a meeting in the morning. Although they knew the meeting's purpose, they needed to determine who Mr. Clarke would select. Fredrick was confident he had been chosen, having asked his sister to plead for him. However, Mr. Clarke and his wife had decided that Alimamy was the appropriate person for the mission, seeing it as an opportunity for him to overcome his past challenges and improve his life.

Mr. Clarke addressed the apprentices, reading the letter for the third time and expressing his happiness about the opportunity. After some delay, he announced, "For the trip to Manchester, I have selected Alimamy."

The shop momentarily fell silent, then erupted in excitement, especially from Alimamy, who expressed immense gratitude to Mr. Clarke.

From his selection to his departure on December 28, 1975, time seemed to fly. Everyone was anxious to see him off. Mr. Clarke and his family accompanied him, boarded the Madam Yoko ferry to Tagrin Ferry Terminal, and then drove to the airport. Alimamy smoothly went through Customs and Immigration and waited in the Departure Lounge. The plane landed at 16:45, and after boarding the SN Brussels aircraft at 17:30, a flight attendant assisted him with his seatbelt. Despite initial fear, Alimamy managed to control his emotions.

Upon reaching Belgium's airspace, the pilot announced the plane's landing in about one hour at the Brussels airport. Later, he realized that adverse weather conditions prevented him from seeing the runway. Eventually, after about thirty minutes, the pilot was asked to land at Zaventem International Airport in Belgium. They spent roughly an hour there and returned to Brussels after the weather had subsided.

Alimamy and the other passengers boarded British Airways for Heathrow Airport in London. The temperature was seven degrees Celsius, which caused Alimamy to shiver. During his interaction with the immigration and customs formalities, he was impatient. He wanted to complete the process as quickly as possible, as he felt cold, thinking it was due to the cooling system in the hall.

As soon as he finished, he hurried out of the hall, hoping to catch some hot air. To his dismay, the temperature outside was only two degrees Celsius. He raised his head, looking at the cloudy sky to ascertain he was outside.

At the end of the long corridor, Alimamy saw a white man holding a placard that read his name. As he walked towards him, he found himself shivering and started to have a runny nose. He joined him and introduced himself to the man, who called himself Neil, and they walked to a station Landover. On reaching the vehicle, a bald, middle-aged man got out, helped Alimamy with his luggage, and took it to the vehicle's boot. They drove to Manchester. Neil's accent was challenging for Alimamy to understand, so he pretended to be tired and sleepy.

The villa was exquisitely unique, with a garden of beautiful flowers scattered around the compound. As Alimamy came down from the vehicle, he saw another tall, ageable man who resembled Neil standing on the house's veranda. The man was Mr. McDonald, and he seemed very happy to see him. He began smiling at him until they reached him, and he warmly hugged Alimamy.

All three of them began chatting about his flight, and later, Mr. McDonald began asking him questions about Mr. Clarke and his experience in the tailoring profession. He later said Neil was the heir to his property, as he was his only child. Mr. McDonald also talked about his late wife, Martha, who died ten years ago from breast cancer. It was sad when Mr. McDonald was talking about his wife, and Alimamy could sense from his expression the grief and pain he must have felt when she died. Without a doubt, he must have loved and cherished his wife.

During their conversation, he explained his experience with Mr. Clark when they were both apprentices in Glasgow under the watchful eyes of Mr. Johnson at Designer Boutique. Later, another young man in his thirties ushered Alimamy into his bedroom, which was self-contained with a toilet. Alimamy was still feeling cold, so he took a hot bath and joined the McDonald's for dinner.

At the time of Alimamy's arrival in Manchester, the McDonald family was taking a break from work for a few days. Yet, he was shown to all of their business establishments and introduced to the managers by Mr. Eddie McDonald's as his adopted son from Africa, which brought him much respect. McDonald quickly regularized his documents permitting Alimamy to work in the country. He and his son Neil were accommodating and friendly; they took Alimamy as part of their family. Of course, he was involved in every discussion and was always asked to contribute to every decision-making.

Twelve days after he arrived, they started operations at the factory. Alimamy was highly impressed to see all types of machines that could make work easier and faster. At the factory, they spent less than an hour sewing one coat suit, while back in Sierra Leone, Mr. Clarke would take about three days to complete a suit because of the unavailability of modern machines. He was fortunate to be taught how to sew other fashion outfits for women, such as wedding dresses, party dresses, evening gowns, jumpers, etc.

During his skills training, he realized that cutting the material to make a design was essential. One has to be creative in sewing women's dresses because women are more fashionable and like new clothes with new designs. He had a passion and became familiar with all the machines. In nine months, he was promoted to Line Manager responsible for designing.

Imagine that Arts and Crafts was not Alimamy 's favorite subject in school. Now that he was considering becoming a Professional Designer and Dress Maker, sketching and drawing designs were relevant. He did everything possible to improve in that area and worked hard. Mr. McDonald and his son, Neil, were impressed with Alimamy's progress, and he was considered a good team player. On his part, Alimamy was motivated to do his utmost.

After three years of dedicated service in Manchester, he was made manager of one of the factories in Scotland. Within two years, he increased the profit margin by up to twenty percent; his branch made the most significant sales for four years. He increased sales by concentrating on women's fashions, which were less expensive to sew but were highly demanding.

While supplying one of the wholesalers during his business engagements, he met Lisa, who later became his wife. They dated for nineteen months, after which he proposed to her because she was pregnant with their first child, Idrissa. That was the name of his late nephew, Hawa's son, who died in that horrible accident with the rest of the family. For their wedding, Alimamy invited both Mr. and Mrs. Clark, but ill health prevented Mr. Clark from attending. Mrs. Clark witnessed the occasion, which was colorful, and was asked to stay with the couple for almost eighteen months to help Lisa look after the newborn.

Lisa and Alimamy had three children: Idrissa, Ami (named after his late biological mother), and Neil (named after his adopted brother). Their relationship was perfect, with Lisa being delectable, a real friend, and lovable. He had no business looking at other women.

He and his family spent most of their vacations visiting museums and other historical places of interest around Europe. Although Lisa was beautiful and sophisticated, she had never been extravagant and would always want to approve of how Alimamy spent money. Her annoyance about him wanting to pay his tithes occasionally upset him, and they sometimes argue about it. Also, they always disagreed about assisting his former colleagues back home, but he would do what he thought was right.

On their next vacation, Alimamy and Lisa decided to go to New York for a change with their children. On Wednesday, December 21, 1984, they drove to the Airport and parked their car in one of the "long-stay" parking bays. While they were waiting at the departure lounge for the flight to New York, there was an announcement from the terminal saying, "Ladies and gentlemen, there is an urgent call for Mr. Alimamy Bangalie to report at Manchester Royal Infirmary Hospital on Oxford Road. His brother Neil McDonald had sustained a terrible car accident, and his presence is urgently needed at the hospital. Thanks for your acknowledgment." End of announcement.

He was baffled, not knowing what to do or where to start. He had already made hotel reservations and paid for a three-week suite in the Times Square Tower hotel in New York. He wanted to ignore the call, but his wife persuaded him to attend to Neil and later meet them in New York. He did not wait to see them off. He hastily left the Airport and drove to the hospital.

Upon arrival, he went to the receptionist's desk and enquired about Neil, and he was directed to the Intensive Care Unit. Unfortunately, Neil had already been taken to the theatre for an emergency operation, so he decided to go to the theatre, where he met Ruth, Neil's wife, in the corridor outside the theatre, in a state of shock. He sympathized with her, as she needed someone to comfort her. They asked the doctors and nurses passing in the corridor about Neil's status, but they could not tell them anything substantial.

Less than ten minutes after entering the hospital, he saw a crowd of people running within it, which caught Alimamy's attention. Of course, he was curious to know what had happened. He went to inquire, and upon reaching the receptionist's desk, he heard an older woman talking about a plane crash. He asked her "where the incident occurred," but she did not reply, as she was crying and busy putting some items into her bag.

He could not understand, so he hurried to his car and turned on the radio; he heard the tragic news that traumatized his life forever. It was terrible when he heard the broadcaster say, "Flight No. 477 heading for New York had crashed. There were no survivors; all passengers and crew on board had been killed." Alimamy had lost his wife and three children, and he would have been a casualty, but for the will of God, he was still alive with a heavy heart.

He could not imagine losing his entire family for the second time. What a tragedy! The memory of his parents, sisters, and nephew came fresh to his mind, and tears began running down his cheeks. He started thinking all sorts of negative things: why has God been so wicked and unfair to him? Where had he done wrong, or did his father do something wrong to someone to warrant such a disaster? Were there curses upon his family? He cried and cried. He then took some napkins from the dashboard, wiped his tears, got out of the car, and went back to the hospital, but could not see Ruth, Neil's wife.

On his way out into the parking lot, he saw Ruth approaching him with tears on her face. He thought something had happened to Neil, so he asked her, "How is Neil?" but she was still crying. He asked for the second time, "What had happened?" she was still crying while replying, "Have you not heard the news about the plane crash?" Alimamy did not utter a word but held Ruth closer to his chest and began consoling her as if she had suffered more than him.

Later, they left the car park and went to see Neil. On their way, Ruth asked him questions regarding his family, but he could not comprehend what she was saying; the words seemed to pass through his head. He did not say a word because he was still in a state of shock. Upon reaching the theatre, they discovered Neil had been transferred to one of the private wards.

Neil was unconscious; his forehead and left hand were wrapped in a white bandage. To get first-hand information on the condition, Ruth and Alimamy decided to see the doctor who operated on him. The doctor was a slim British Indian called Pereira, who told them that Neil had a fractured skull and a broken arm, which had been fixed, and there was no cause for alarm.

Alimamy left Ruth at Neil's bedside to go to the crash site. It was horrible to see the debris of the plane scattered on the ground, killing all two hundred and seventy-five passengers and crew members. It was unbearable, his body was covered with sweat, and he began crying again.

There were many other people at the site; some were trying to see if they could find their loved ones, others were journalists with cameras all around, and others were security personnel who were vigilant, ensuring people were not interfering with the wreckage and did not allow anyone to get closer to the accident site. That evening, when he went home, he found himself fading, weak, and hopeless; he fell asleep on the sofa in the living room.

The following day, it was Ruth who woke him up. She was sad and deeply sympathized with him and brought him some food, but he had no appetite. He made himself a cup of coffee, which he drank, and then they left to see Mr. Eddie McDonald, who had been suffering from partial paralysis. His countenance was gloomy. They did not explain anything about Neil's car accident or the plane crash because it could have affected his health.

After a while, he and Ruth left for the crash site, where they met a crowd of investigators. They did not spend much time at the scene, as they could not get helpful information. They returned to the hospital, where Neil was lying on his back. His eyes were open, and he recognized them. They talked about his car accident and expressed their sympathy without mentioning anything concerning the plane crash.

Fortunately for Alimamy, the bodies of his beautiful and beloved wife and children were recovered from the wreckage. Ten days after the police had concluded their investigation and upon the completion of autopsy reports, he was called by the police to identify the corpses of his family. His wife was buried in her wedding dress, which he had designed and sewn for her, while his children wore their school ceremonial uniforms. The ceremony was colorful but heart-breaking, and with this situation, Alimamy's entire life appeared empty and hopeless.

As a way of dealing with his grief, he decided to return home to Sierra Leone to engage in some philanthropic activity. He contacted friends in Sierra Leone to create a relevant platform. By then, Mr. Clarke, \\a significantly older man, could not help him with his proposed projects.

Brima Rogers, his friend at Ahmadiyya Secondary School, Bo, was willing and prepared to assist him. Brima, a University of Sierra Leone graduate with a division one degree in Economics, later earned an ACCA from the University of Washington, USA. On his return to Sierra Leone, he became a finance officer for one of the NGOs in Bo Town. They discussed several projects, one of which was the establishment of an orphanage in Bo to reduce the number of orphans roaming the streets of Bo who could become victims of social menace.

Four months after Neil was discharged from the hospital, Alimamy asked for a meeting with him and his dad. The meeting was centered on his decision to return to Sierra Leone. He told them he was unhappy living in the United Kingdom, having no one to share his dreams with. He then narrated the fatal accident in which he lost his parents and siblings, which left him alone and destitute at an early age. With God's grace, he was privileged and fortunate to reach that far with the help of people who had love and fear of God. It's about time he went home to pay back to those now in a similar position he was about twenty years ago.

It was the first time Alimamy had explained his life's challenges to anyone. You could sense their empathy for him, prompting Neil and his father to pledge one hundred thousand pounds each to establish his philanthropic organization and give him a twenty percent stake in their company.

Amazingly, wealth or riches were no longer critical to Alimamy. Although he was not a rich man, he had a burning desire to put smiles on the faces of others. The only way he could accomplish this was to contribute meaningfully to the social and economic well-being of the less privileged, especially the vulnerable children in his motherland.

CHAPTER EIGHT

GOING BACK HOME

Ninety days after meeting with the McDonald family, Alimamy returned to Sierra Leone, determined to start his projects and aid the less fortunate. Before heading back, he considered visiting the Gambia. Many friends had spoken highly of the Gambian people's hospitality, and he felt he could learn from their experiences.

Three days before departing from the UK, Alimamy traveled from Manchester to London to get a landing visa from the Gambian High Commission Office on Oxford Street. His friendly demeanor with the officials ensured he was quickly served, spending less than fifteen minutes at the office. Afterward, he bought an air ticket for Freetown via Banjul at Gambian Airlines on Rocklin

Street, opting for an open ticket to extend his stay if needed.

During his three nights in London, Alimamy stayed at the Westbridge Hotel. He spent his time watching movies, swimming in the hotel pool, or sitting by the pool watching visitors. Before leaving London, he reserved a room and paid in advance at the Seaview Garden Hotel in Gambia. On July 17, 1985, at about 11:30 am, he left the Westbridge Hotel and traveled by underground train to Heathrow Airport. After checking in and going through immigration, he waited in the departure lounge, his mind occupied with the challenges awaiting him in Sierra Leone.

In the lounge, Alimamy noticed that most passengers bound for The Gambia were tourists, excited about their journey. The Gambian Airlines flight arrived at about 12:45 pm, bringing back tourists dressed in Gambian attire. He watched the Jet A-1 fuel truck refuel the plane. Shortly after, the announcement for boarding was made.

As the passengers boarded, a flight attendant in a Gambian uniform welcomed them with a smile, "Good afternoon, ladies and gentlemen. This is Air Gambia Flight 407, and if it's your first time joining our flight, you are highly welcome." She continued, "This is a direct flight to Banjul, the Gambia; the estimated arrival time is five hours and forty-five minutes."

As the plane took off, Alimamy felt a rush of adrenaline. Once they reached cruising altitude, an air hostess announced lunch service. Alimamy ordered a hamburger with a can of Coke. Upon reaching Gambian airspace, the pilot announced their imminent descent and estimated arrival time. Alimamy watched the landscape below, captivated by the Atlantic Ocean, scattered trees, and flowing rivers.

The flight landed smoothly, and as the plane taxied to the gate, the hostess thanked the passengers for choosing Gambian Airlines. When Alimamy exited the plane, he was impressed by the airport's construction but noticed the officers' vigilant eyes.

A Seaview Garden Hotel officer held a placard with Alimamy Bangalie's name. As soon as Alimamy saw it, he greeted him. The gentleman, Balamusa N'jai, introduced himself and helped Alimamy with his luggage. During the drive to the hotel, Balamusa shared that he was married with two children and offered to be available for any assistance during Alimamy's stay.

The Seaview Garden Hotel, located along the Atlantic Ocean, uniquely appealed to tourists. On his first day at the hotel, Alimamy relaxed on the veranda, enjoying the pleasant weather. A clear view of the beach from his room entertained him until he decided to visit a nightclub downtown.

Two days later, after taking in the sights around the hotel, he requested Balamusa's assistance to tour Banjul's cultural and heritage sites. They visited the National Museum, the Presidential Office, and the Courthouse, although security prevented entry to the State House.

Their tour included visits to architecturally impressive mosques and a peanut factory in Serrekunda, managed by Alhaji Abu-Bakar Sal. Mr. Sal shared insights into his business's challenges and successes, highlighting the impact of fluctuating product prices.

After sightseeing, Alimamy and Balamusa returned to the hotel, enjoyed a delicious dinner, and decided to visit a nightclub. That night, Balamusa took Alimamy to Aquarius along the Senegambia Strip Kololi. The club was vibrant and filled with women from various West African countries.

The lady sitting by him noticed his interest, watching a bouncing lady walking toward the bar. She held him by his chin and kissed him, but Alimamy's thoughts were still on the bouncing lady, which made him a bit nervous.

Immediately, he told Balamusa to call the lady, which he did, but the lady refused to come. She told Balamusa, "If he wants to talk to me, tell him to come over." "Okay," Balamusa replied. As soon as he conveyed her message to Alimamy, he got to his feet and went to the lady.

When they started talking, her voice reminded him of someone he had known before but could not remember, probably because of the flashing disco lights, which camouflaged everyone's appearance. Curiously, he asked, "Could we talk outside? " She instantly agreed and nodded her head.

After many years without seeing or thinking of Satta, it was a surprise and an almost million-to-one chance to meet her again for the second time. As soon as they left the club, he realized that the lady was no other than Satta Konneh, his girlfriends from Koindu Agricultural Secondary School, whom he had not seen for a long time. Satta, too, was quick to recognize him. They hugged passionately, and she began crying, without knowing why, and he started consoling her. She laid her head on his shoulder as a sign of assurance. Alimamy introduced Satta and Balamusa and told Balamusa that they should return to the hotel.

On reaching the hotel, Alimamy squeezed some money into Balamusa's hand to express his appreciation.

On entering the hotel lobby, he was confronted by the Bar Manager: "Hello, Mr. Bangalie. Can I have a talk with you for a moment?" "No problem," Alimamy replied, waving his hand to Satta to wait for him in the lobby. He then entered the manager's office.

The manager asked him a series of questions about Satta without waiting for any reply. "Sorry for intruding into your personal affairs, but management must be cautious about our client's well-being and safety." He paused momentarily, looking through the window to ascertain Satta would not hear him. He continued, "Anyway, sir, where did you meet that lady? As Alimamy wanted to reply, he continued, "Have you met her before, Mr. Bangalie? It's risky meeting some of these ladies; they can steal, so you have to be very careful with your property. Of course, there are some condoms in the bed left drawer if one is needed." He then paused as if waiting for an answer.

At this point, he looked at Alimamy as if he had committed a serious crime. The young man replied, "Oh no. Mr. Manager, I've known her for quite a long time; she was my." But the manager interrupted him, "Okay! I see Mr. Bangalie. That's good news, but remember to secure yourself. "I will, Mr. Manager," he replied and left the office.

Satta had already settled at the receptionist's desk, relaxing and enjoying the song "Many Rivers to Cross" by Jimmy Cliff. Alimamy went to the bar and ordered food and drinks for the two of them to be served in his room. They went to his room and waited patiently for the order, which allowed them privacy.

After about twenty minutes, the room service order was brought: shrimp, lobster, and a bottle of Champagne. Before eating, Satta held his hand, and they went into the bathroom for a cold shower. It was the first time Alimamy realized how affectionate and sexy Satta was when she laid her naked skin against his. He felt the tenderness on her breasts, especially when her nipples were bobbling against his hairy chest. He couldn't ignore God's creation by his side. He suddenly found his tongue in her mouth, kissing her. Her fair complexion was immaculate under the blue light that kept him mesmerized.

They spent ample time in the bathroom, having fun with great excitement. After bathing, Alimamy noticed Satta wanted more of him but thought they needed to eat their food. He gave her one of his dressing robes to wear while he put on his pajamas, ready to celebrate this special occasion. After that, they went out to the balcony, where he popped the bottle of Champagne. While eating and drinking, they began discussing.

However, Alimamy was curious about what had prompted her to go to Gambia, so he asked her. She got silent, which ignited Alimamy's thought that her past might not have been pleasant. She began talking about her hurtful experience with her father and stepmother, which made her move away and stay with one of her friends; it was during this period that she got pregnant in Grade Eleven, but she continued her schooling in the evenings and later gave birth to a boy named Mustapha.

Still, her problem increased as her son's father was irresponsible and had little choice but to engage in prostitution. She got pregnant again, this time by a Korean fisherman, and later delivered a girl child named Marion. The Korean was very caring but later left Liberia without informing her, which shattered her hopes.

Satta said her burden was tremendous, leaving her suspicious of all men who had come around for a relationship because they were not interested in caring for her children. After that, she left her children with her grandmother, who lived in Magibi County in Liberia. She had traveled to the Gambia looking for a relationship that might lead to stability in life.

As she explained, she felt sorry for herself, and tears began running down her cheeks. She left Alimamy sitting on the porch and ran into the bedroom. He followed her and began to console her; he told her not to lose hope but to focus on a brighter future with the two of them. She was shocked when she heard those words, and knowing Alimamy's sincerity, she felt relief that her dreams had finally been achieved.

Her excitement was overwhelming, but she was quick to hide her feelings; she asked him about his family, but he did not answer as he tried to avoid discussing the tragic death of his family, which always disturbed him. She continued to ask the same question without a reply and quickly noticed that his countenance had changed. So, she then asked him, "Is anything the matter?" He replied, "Yes, there was a terrible accident, and all my family died; I do not like talking about it." "Okay, honey," she said, "too bad, but how did it happen, darling?" He replied, "I'll tell you later; I have no family now." Tears began to run down Satta's cheeks in a show of her empathy. He could not control his emotions; he started explaining his entire life story until both fell asleep.

They woke up at about 9:30 am, and immediately after their bath, he asked the main desk to send someone to come clean the room. In a few minutes, room service cleaned the entire place perfectly. Alimamy wore one of the new jean suits he bought in London while Satta had the same dress she had worn the previous night at the nightclub. As soon as they had breakfast, he took Satta for shopping. She appreciated that he spent roughly five hundred US dollars on her. After shopping, she took him to her house.

It was a one-bedroom, self-contained apartment where she lived with two other girls from Sierra Leone. They were cooking groundnut soup; the aroma was all over the place. She introduced him to the ladies, whose names were Christiana and Halima, and went into their small room to get some of her underwear to go to the hotel. Upon reaching the hotel, Satta tried on all the dresses to see the ones that suited her most.

While undressing, Alimamy's arm mistakenly touched her hip. She immediately pressed her body against his, and he swiftly lifted her and lay her on the bed. It was splendid having someone by your side that you love and, of course, willing to share affection with. He could feel the excitement and vibration from her breath, telling him she was enjoying herself. It was short, but it opened a new adventure in their relationship, which Satta had yearned for long before now. Afterward, they showered and went to the lounge for drinks, where they discussed lengthily on various issues, and finally, Alimamy proposed to marry her. It was a moment Satta had been praying for, but how soon it happened was beyond her expectations.

The next day, they went shopping for their wedding clothes. Hers was a white round-neck gown with long sleeves, a big bow at the back with a refined design of white feathers along the edges of the dress, two white pairs of gloves, a white pair of shoes, a white lady's bag, while Alimamy had a grey three-piece suit with a white shirt, black tie, and a pair of black shoes. Later, they went to Satta's house to inform her friends about their plans. Though her friends were happy about their plans, they were shocked at how quickly things had unfolded. He gave them some money and the address of his friend Brima Rogers in case they happened to visit Freetown, as he didn't have an address at the moment.

CHAPTER NINE

THE WEDDING

At around 11:30 am, Alimamy settled his bill with the hotel manager and handed over his room key. The finality of the gesture felt heavier than expected. With Satta by his side, they departed the hotel in a vehicle provided by Balamusa N'jai, who escorted them to the Gambia International Airport for a flight to Monrovia, Liberia. The air was thick with anticipation as they reached the airport, the start of a significant new chapter.

The security at Roberts International Airport (RIA) in Liberia was imposing. Officers, clad in various uniforms and armed with guns and teargas canisters, patrolled with a vigilance reminiscent of American security forces. Alimamy couldn't help but be struck by the difference in the Liberian accent—a subtle reminder of Liberia's unique historical ties with the United States. He marveled at how a country so distant could echo the familiar.

As they navigated through immigration and customs, the weight of the upcoming wedding loomed large. They hired a taxi for the forty-nine-kilometer drive to Monrovia, but Satta asked the driver to make a detour to her mother's house on VP Road.

Upon arrival, Satta and Alimamy were greeted warmly. Satta introduced Alimamy to her family—her mother, stepfather, Mr. Nathaniel Togbeh, younger stepsisters Victoria and Agnes, and younger brother Patrick. Mama Titi, her mother, seemed pleased yet anxious as she asked, "When are you planning the wedding?"

"This coming Saturday," Satta responded. Victoria's eyes widened in shock. "Wow, this Saturday?" "Yes, Vicky," Satta affirmed. Mama Titi's face tightened with concern. "It's too soon to get prepared." "What do you mean, Mama Titi?" Satta asked, her voice edged with worry. Mama Titi responded bluntly: "We cannot financially support this event right now."

Satta turned to Alimamy, seeking his approval. "I understand your position. Tell us what you people need for the wedding, and we shall make it available." Alimamy nodded in agreement.

Mama Titi's relief was evident as her smile returned. She said, "Now you are talking." They laughed, and she hugged Satta. She continued, "First, we need a family meeting tomorrow with your father and other family members to agree on the arrangements."

Later, they went to her father's house, which was filled with an unsettling quiet. As they arrived, Satta's father, Mr. Konneh, greeted them with palpable hostility. "After six years of silence and unresolved conflict with my wife, what brings you back?"

Satta's silence was a stark contrast to her father's outburst. Alimamy felt the sting of the situation, but he and Satta stood their ground, waiting for Mr. Konneh to address them.

Minutes felt like hours before Mr. Konneh finally spoke to Alimamy. "Mister man, what is the reason for the visit?" Alimamy replied, "Good afternoon; we are here to inform you and your family that Satta and I have decided to marry."

The reaction was immediate. Mr. Konneh's demeanor shifted from calm to authoritative. "So, you only come now because of this marriage plan? You must apologize to my wife for the insult you caused her before your abrupt disappearance. Otherwise, we will not participate in your wedding."

The tension in the air was suffocating. Satta watched in disbelief as her father's anger boiled over. Alimamy stepped in. "On behalf of myself and my fiancée, we appeal to you and your wife to forgive us."

Immediately, Satta knelt before her stepmother, her voice trembling as she asked for forgiveness. Mama Mona accepted the apology and ushered them into the living room to discuss the wedding plans. The family agreed to meet the next day to finalize arrangements at her mother's residence.

The atmosphere starkly contrasted the day's tension at the Clayton Hotel, where Alimamy and Satta stayed. The five-star hotel offered a serene retreat with its city and Atlantic Ocean views. Their room, number forty-two, was a haven of calm. After a quick meal ordered for room service, Alimamy turned on CNN to follow the midterm elections in the United States while Satta drifted asleep.

They met with more of Satta's extended family members at her mother's house the following day. Alimamy was introduced to them. The meeting, delayed by the arrival of Mr. and Mrs. Konneh, eventually began around 11:15 am. Discussions about financial constraints arose, forcing Alimamy to agree to cover the wedding costs, totalling approximately eight thousand United States dollars. The decision was made for a breakfast wedding at 9:30 am at the Registrar General's Office, followed by a reception at the City Hall auditorium. Mama Mona's excitement about the wedding was evident despite the earlier tension.

On the eve of the wedding, there was an Engagement Ceremony, where Alimamy presented Satta with a stunning engagement ring from Gold Finger Jewelries. The twenty-four-carat gold ring, costing one thousand five hundred US dollars, was complemented by a wedding ring, a twenty-four-carat gold band with a thirty-six-carat diamond, worth three thousand US dollars. Alimamy chose to wear the same ring he had used with his late wife, Lisa.

The Engagement Ceremony was lively yet short, but the family insisted that he pay the family a bride price of five thousand US dollars, which he did. Alimamy and Satta also had no contact before the wedding, adding a layer of suspense. Alimamy spent the night at the hotel while Satta stayed at her stepmother's. The anticipation of the wedding made sleep elusive for Alimamy, who was eager for the ceremony to pass so he could focus on new projects. At 6:45 am, two of Satta's cousins, his Best Men, met him at the hotel. They left five minutes before the ceremony and briefly drove around town to calm the nerves.

Arriving at the Registrar General's Office, the suspense was palpable. The Registrar, Mr. David Weah, in his early sixties, officiated the ceremony. Alimamy and Satta exchanged vows and rings, signing the marriage certificate amidst excitement and relief.

The immediate transition to the City Hall Complex for the reception added to the day's whirlwind pace. The auditorium on Tubman Boulevard was bustling with family and friends. Mr. Jefferson Sumo, the Chairman, quickly set the tone, inviting Alimamy to deliver his speech.

Alimamy's voice resonated with heartfelt gratitude and emotion. "Good morning, ladies and gentlemen. On behalf of my wife and I, I want to extend our thanks and appreciation for being here with us to make this day a reality. Special thanks go to my wife's parents for allowing me to meet my beautiful wife. Above all, I thank the Almighty God for bringing us together. We have known each other for over twenty years, and today is a testament to our enduring love. We hope you will continue to remember us in your prayers for God's protection, favor, and blessings. Once more, thank you all, and stay blessed."

The toast to their marriage was met with a resounding cheer, and the reception continued with food, drinks, and speeches. By midday, the wedding festivities concluded. Alimamy and Satta returned to Mama Titi's house for a brief family discussion before returning to the hotel for a peaceful evening.

On Sunday morning, they visited a Pentecostal Church on Bushrod Island. Holy Mother Dura prophesied a bright future for Alimamy and admonished him to glorify God by helping the needy.

Later, they enjoyed a drive through Monrovia, visiting key landmarks like the Executive Mansion, the Capitol Building, and the University of Liberia. Although they had planned to venture out of town, Alimamy's exhaustion led them back to the hotel to rest.

On Monday, Satta's paternal sister, Kadi Konneh, joined them on a trip to their grandmother in Magibi County to collect Satta's children. Despite the potholes and delays, they reached Aunty Catty, Satta's grandmother, who joyfully received them. Her prayers and humor warmed the visit despite the children's tears at their departure.

Alimamy kept his wedding a secret from friends in

Sierra Leone to avoid distractions. They processed the children's birth certificates and travel permits the following day, securing tickets for their journey to Freetown. The flight from Roberts International Airport to Lungi International Airport was uneventful, and upon arrival, they hired a taxi to the Bintumani Hotel.

Alimamy's old friend, Brima Roger, was surprised to learn about his swift remarriage but understood his plight. They briefly discussed Alimamy's project and agreed to meet in Bo Town to actualize it. After spending three days relaxing with his family and visiting Mr. and Mrs. Clark, Alimamy ensured they were well-stocked with groceries from Choitrams Supermarket before heading to Bo.

CHAPTER TEN

TRIP TO BO

The following morning, on Saturday, 15 February 1985, at about 6:30 a.m., Alimamy took his brief-case containing a few clothes that Satta had packed, some money, and documents about his proposed project. He left his family sleeping and set off for Bo Town. Racing down the hotel's steps, he boarded a hired taxi to the bus station. He would have preferred the Jeep for his trip to Bo, but being a survivor of a gruesome accident, the memory always haunted him. Thus, he opted for the Government Bus.

Two notorious criminals at the bus station seemed to be fooling aimlessly. Momoh and Tamba had just been released from jail after completing a sentence for aggra-vated robbery with violence. Best friends and inseparable in their illicit activities, they had no permanent address and moved between Sierra Leone's significant towns, including the Airport, scouting for passengers to trail and to rob.

On that day, they left Freetown for Bo, trailing Alimamy to rob him after gathering information about his financial status. At the bus station, there was a long queue of passengers vying for tickets. While queuing, a hustler approached Alimamy, offering to sell him one ticket at a slightly higher price. He bought the ticket to avoid waiting in the queue and immediately boarded the bus, taking seat number twenty-four.

Later, the hustler, who seemed to be a conspirator, approached Momoh and Tamba and issued ticket numbers twenty-five and twenty-six. Minutes later, the passengers filled their seats, and the driver sounded the horn, signaling readiness to depart.

During this period, the two men, Tamba and Momoh, well-dressed in their mid-thirties, rushed toward the bus, carrying a briefcase similar to Alimamy's. They hurried inside the bus; Momoh sat on the aisle side of Alimamy, while Tamba was seated on the aisle adjacent to Momoh.

Next, a uniformed man entered, inspecting each ticket for authenticity. After confirming them, he wished the driver and passengers a safe trip and left.

Alimamy remembered seeing someone like Momoh at Lungi International Airport on his return to Sierra Leone. During that moment, Momoh was chasing a diamond businessman but was disrupted by the presence of Airport police officers.

Momoh and Tamba spoke loudly, disturbing the peace of their fellow passengers. Alimamy fell asleep, and they seized the opportunity to switch his briefcase with theirs and anxiously awaited to get off the bus at the next stop.

At Moyamba Junction, the driver halted for a toilet and refreshment break. All passengers, except Alimamy and an older man, who were both fast asleep, stayed on the bus. Both male and female Sellers of all ages swarmed around the bus with various foods, fruits, sugary drinks, water, and vegetables, praising the commodities or goods they were selling. Alimamy later woke up and called a banana vendor, but several children rushed to him, shouting, "Yes sir! Please buy my own ...." He confirmed his choice and transacted with the original boy, telling him to keep the change, then generously gave money to the others. They reciprocated by offering him their goods, but he refused.

Half an hour later, the driver sounded the horn so that

passengers could come back onboard and proceed with the journey. All passengers reboarded except Momoh and Tamba, who had escaped with Alimamy's briefcase, which was unknown to him at the resumption of the journey. Despite the delay, the driver waited an additional ten minutes before continuing. Some passengers, familiar with Momoh and Tamba, discussed their criminal behavior. Alimamy checked in the locker for his bag, saw it, and was reassured.

When he arrived at the Bo bus station, his friend Brima Rogers was waiting. Shocked, Alimamy discovered his bag was heavier than expected. Opening it, he found only old clothes, books, newspapers, and stones. He was speechless and started shivering and sweating profusely, realizing Momoh and Tamba's mischief. Brima urged him to report the theft to the police immediately. They drove to the Police Station at the junction of Dambala Road in Brima's car.

The policeman at the station desk, Sergeant Marah, logged the incident in their ledger at the station. He confirmed he knew Momoh and Tamba very well. As he described his suspects, the Sergeant took pictures from a drawer beside him, handed them to Alimamy, and asked, "Can you identify anyone from those pictures?" There was a bit of silence in the office while Alimamy was going through the pictures until he suddenly said, "Yes, these are the guys who dropped at Moyamba Junction," pointing to the images and showing the photos to his friend Brima. After that, Sgt. Marah left Alimamy and Brima with his colleagues, who were talking to Alimamy to get more information from him.

Sgt. Marah went in the direction of what was believed to be the radio room. In less than five minutes, he returned and said that he had sent radio messages to all stations around the country for the immediate arrest of the two suspects.

Alimamy left the police station that evening with mixed feelings, whether the police would conspire with the suspects after apprehension or if they would act professionally and diligently to prosecute them. He, however, did not allow his feelings to cause a hasty conclusion on the matter and tried hard to focus on other issues. Later, they left and went to Brima's house.

Brima's wife, Aminata, greeted them warmly, eager to meet Alimamy. She noticed his lack of luggage and expressed concern. Brima explained Alimamy's predicament, and Aminata insisted they get him some clothes. Brima took money from their bedroom drawer and left with Alimamy to buy essentials.

Returning, Alimamy showered and joined the Rogers

family for dinner. He worried about how to tell his wife, Satta, about the lost money. She had advised him not to travel with such much money, but he had ignored her advice. He decided not to call her that night but would do so after receiving police progress in the morning.

Meanwhile, Satta couldn't sleep, anxious about Alimamy's silence. She consulted the hotel management twice, and they reassured her there was no accident on the Freetown to Bo Road. Despite this, she remained restless, recalling the tragic deaths of Alimamy's parents, first wife Lisa, and children.

At 1:30 am, Alimamy tried calling Satta, but she was in the bath. A hotel staff member went to inform her, but Satta slipped and injured herself while rushing to the door. Her son found her unconscious and bleeding, prompting the hotel to rush her to the Emergency Unit at the Connaught Government Hospital. Alimamy was informed of her accident and grew more anxious and worried.

Satta's injury was not serious. After treatment, she was discharged and returned to the hotel. She learned that Alimamy was safe and had been trying to reach her. Immediately, she called him.

"Good morning, mummy; how are you feeling now?"

Alimamy asked. Ignoring his question, she asked, "What happened? You didn't call yesterday." "We arrived late and didn't want to disturb you and the children," he explained. "So, how are things going with you?" she inquired. "Not bad," he answered, asking about her health. "I'm feeling better, just missing you," she admitted.

"Me too, darling," Alimamy responded. "I plan to return today due to your injury." "No need for alarm. I'm quite okay now," she assured him. "Please handle the money carefully and trust no one. People are deceptive." Alimamy couldn't hide the incident any longer. "Mummy, I lost my briefcase yesterday," he confessed.

"What did you say?" she asked in disbelief. "I lost my briefcase yesterday," he repeated. Furious, she demanded an explanation. Alimamy promised to explain upon his return, adding that the police were on the case. "Forget about that money," she replied, skeptical of the African police. Despite her doubts, Alimamy reassured her of the police's commitment to recovering the money. "I wish you the best, honey. Hope to see you soon," she said. "Love you all, and bye for now," he replied.

The following day, Alimamy and Brima visited the police station. Officer-in-Charge Samuel Williams informed them of the ongoing search for Momoh and

Tamba. Alimamy asked for an update, but the officer could not provide a definite timeline and urged patience.

Brima, who didn't work on Saturdays, took Alimamy to inspect the land he had purchased for an orphanage. The flat plot near the town center was perfect. They visited three construction companies for cost estimates and planned a multi-purpose building with extensive facilities.

Five days later, they received bids from Bright and Kanu Construction Company and Apex Construction and Engineering Company. Despite Apex's lower cost, they chose Bright and Kanu because of their credibility. Hundreds, including the Resident Minister of the Southern Province, attended the groundbreaking ceremony.

After the ceremony, Alimamy hired a vehicle back to Freetown, constantly cautioning the driver to reduce his speed when he exceeded the stipulated speed limit on the road. At the hotel, a receptionist informed him that his family was at the swimming pool. Alimamy hurried to join them. Satta was lying on a camp bed reading a newspaper while the children were swimming. The children greeted him enthusiastically, and eager for answers, Satta asked about the briefcase. Alimamy recounted the entire episode, and Satta, though sympathetic, couldn't hide her frustration. He reassured her of the police's efforts to recover the money and urged her not to worry.

A seventeen-year-old girl, Kumba, who lived in Tokeh, had left home for twenty-eight hours without her family knowing her whereabouts. The family searched for her, and she was found in the company of Tamba and Momoh, but she refused to go home. Due to her refusal, the family contacted the police. The police instantly sent a plain-clothes CID officer to investigate the matter. Upon his arrival at the scene, he noticed Tamba and Momoh but pretended to be a relative of the young girl, swaying her to go home, but she insisted.

This was a blessing in disguise. Eleven days after the theft, the police learned about Momoh and Tamba's whereabouts. Upon returning to the station, the officer informed his superiors of Tamba and Momoh's location. They immediately informed CID headquarters in Freetown about their suspects' location. A team of plain-clothes officers from Freetown CID headquarters, led by Inspector Yankar Sesay, was dispatched to execute the arrest.

Upon their arrival at Tokeh Police Station, they strate-gized their approach. Dividing into five groups, they surrounded their target from different angles. Momoh and Tamba, completely drunk, were quickly arrested along with other people who were on the scene. Despite attempts to bribe the officers, they were all, including Kumba, handcuffed and taken to CID for interrogation.

During the interrogation, Kumba and the other young girls were released. The suspects' confessions were documented, revealing additional stolen items in Bo, hidden by one of their accomplices, Ahmed Kamara. They admitted to various thefts, and the police recovered a significant portion of the stolen money. Alimamy was summoned to the CID office to identify his belongings. He recognized his clothes, though other items were missing. The suspects were charged and taken to court.

The accused, remanded at Pademba Road Prison, faced trial. The Judge thoroughly questioned the Prosecution and Defence Teams and heard testimonies from several witnesses. Alimamy recounted his loss, and the officers described the arrests. Their Defence counsel's attempt to discredit Alimamy's claims was unsuccessful.

After concluding statements, the Judge found Momoh and Tamba guilty and sentenced them to five years imprisonment with hard labor. Ahmed Kamara was sentenced to six months imprisonment for possession of stolen property. The verdict relieved Alimamy and his family as the remaining money found on the culprits was returned to him. The Judge later advised him to be cautious with his personal belongings, especially when traveling on public transport.

Months later, Alimamy continued to expand his business. Despite the trauma, he remained vigilant, avoiding unnecessary risks. He learned valuable lessons in trust and caution, fortifying his resolve to protect his family's future.

THE EXPANSION AND REUNION

Weeks turned to months and months to years, and Alimamy's business flourished. His resilience and determination finally paid off, leading to the successful establishment of the Orphanage in Bo. The facility, named Hope of Haven, became a sanctuary for orphans from all over the country. It provided education, healthcare, and a nurturing environment, embodying Alimamy's vision of giving back to the community.

The groundbreaking ceremony was a milestone, but the real work began afterward. Construction crews worked tirelessly, adhering to the plans drawn up by Bright and Kanu Construction Company. Alimamy oversaw the progress, ensuring that every detail met his high standards. The multi-purpose residential building comprised classrooms, dormitories, a library, a play-ground, and a healthcare unit.

The first batch of orphans arrived in January and were greeted by a team of dedicated staff. Alimamy, often accompanied by Satta and their children, visited frequently. They bonded with the children, sharing meals, stories, and laughter. The orphanage became a second home filled with joy and hope.

Alimamy's business ventures continued to grow. He expanded into real estate, acquiring properties all over the country. His investments yielded significant returns, which he reinvested into the community. He funded scholarships, supported local businesses, and initiated programs to empower women and youth.

Alimamy's success brought stability and prosperity to his family. His children excelled in their studies, inspired by their father's achievements and generosity. Satta, always by his side, managed the family's affairs with grace and wisdom. She remained his confidante and pillar of strength, guiding him through challenges and cele-brating victories.

On the orphanage's first anniversary, members of the Bo community were invited to grace the occasion. Due to the high humidity, the event was held on the football pitch. Standing under the shade of a large mango tree, he addressed the crowd. "Today, we celebrate not only the success of Hope of Haven but also the beginning of a new chapter," his voice filled with emotion. "I am proud to announce the establishment of "The Ami Bangalie Foundation" in memory of my mother. This foundation will continue our mission of supporting those in need, providing accommodation, education, healthcare, and opportunities for a better life."

The crowd erupted in applause, their faces beaming with pride and gratitude. Satta joined him on stage, and together, they unveiled the foundation's logo, a symbol of hope and unity.

Despite his success, Alimamy never forgot his ordeal with Momoh and Tamba. The experience left him more cautious and empathetic towards those driven to desperation by poverty and lack of opportunity. He initiated programs within the foundation to rehabilitate former criminals, providing them with skills training and employment opportunities.

One day, as Alimamy was reviewing applications for the rehabilitation program, a familiar name caught his eye— Ahmed Kamara. The memory of the stolen briefcase and the police raid in Bo flooded back. Intrigued, he decided to meet Ahmed personally.

In a small, dimly lit room at the foundation's office, Ahmed awaited his fate. When Alimamy entered, he stood, his eyes filled with fear and remorse." Mr. Bah," he stammered, "I... I never thought I would see you again."

Alimamy regarded him calmly. "I believe in second chances, Ahmed. You have an opportunity here to turn your life around. But it will require hard work, dedication, and honesty." Ahmed nodded fervently, tears welling up in his eyes. "Thank you, sir. I won't let you down."

The Ami Bangalie Foundation became a beacon of hope and transformation as the years passed. Its initiatives touched thousands of lives, and Alimamy's resilience, compassion, and generosity legacy endured.

In his twilight years, Alimamy reflected on his journey. From the harrowing experiences after the death of his parents and siblings, coupled with the death of his first wife and children, to the triumphant establishment of Hope of Haven and the Ami Bangalie foundation, he realized that every challenge had shaped him into the man he had become. His life's work was a testament to the power of perseverance, faith, love, and the unwavering belief in one's self for a better tomorrow.

Surrounded by his family, friends, and the children he had helped, Alimamy knew that he had fulfilled his destiny. His story was one of redemption and renewal, a journey that had come full circle, leaving an indelible mark on the world and the lives he had touched.

www.ingramcontent.com/pod-product-compliance
Lightning Source LLC
Chambersburg PA
CBHW071445130726

47997CB00006B/2230